for

MARY LINDLEY STEERE

Harper Trophy® is a registered trademark
of HarperCollins Publishers Inc.

Library of Congress Catalog Card Number: 58-5292
ISBN 0-06-020991-7 (lib. bdg.)
ISBN 0-06-440250-9 (pbk.)
First Harper Trophy edition, 1989.
❖

The Family

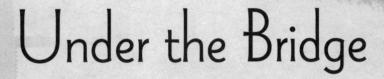

Under the Bridge

NATALIE SAVAGE CARLSON

Pictures by GARTH WILLIAMS

HarperTrophy®
A Division of HarperCollins*Publishers*

Chapter One

Once there was an old hobo named Armand who wouldn't have lived anywhere but in Paris. So that is where he lived.

Everything that he owned could be pushed around in an old baby buggy without any hood, so he had no worries about rents or burglars. All the ragged clothing he owned was on his back, so he didn't need to bother with trunks or dry-cleaners.

It was easy for him to move from one hidey-hole to another so that is what he was doing one late morning in December. It was a cold day with the gray sky hanging on the very chimney pots of Paris. But Armand did not mind because he had a tickly feeling that something new and exciting was going to happen to him today.

He hummed a gay tune to himself as he pushed his buggy through the flower market at the side of Notre Dame cathedral. The flowers reminded him that someday it would be spring even though it wasn't bad winter yet.

There were pots of fragile hyacinths and tulips crowded together on planks in front of the stalls. There were pink carnations and oleanders in great tin pails. Most of all there were bouquets of red-beaded holly, clumps of white-pearled mistletoe and little green fir trees because it would soon be Christmas.

Armand's keen eye caught sight of a pile of broken branches and wilted flowers swept away from one stall. "Anabel" was the name written over the stall, and Armand touched his black beret to the stocky woman whose blue work apron hung below her wooly coat.

"By your leave and in gratitude for your

generosity, madame," he said to the woman who was surely Anabel. He piled the broken branches on top of his belongings in the baby buggy. Then he fastidiously picked a sprig of dried holly from the litter and pulled it through his torn buttonhole. He wanted to look his best for whatever gay adventure was waiting for him this day.

The woman who must have been Anabel only frowned at Armand as he trundled his buggy toward the Rue de Corse. Past the ancient buildings he shuffled, his buggy headed for the far branch of the Seine River.

But as he entered the square in front of Notre Dame, a hand grasped his arm from behind.

"Your fortune, monsieur," wheedled a musical voice. "You will meet with adventure today."

Armand let go of the handle of the buggy and whirled around to face a gypsy woman in a short fur coat and full, flowered skirt.

He gave her a gap-toothed smile. "You,

Mireli," he greeted her. "Your people are back in Paris for the winter?"

The gypsy woman's dark face beamed under the blue scarf. "Doesn't one always spend the winters in Paris?" she asked, as if she were a woman of fashion. "But have you taken to the streets so early?"

Armand shrugged his shoulders under the long overcoat that almost reached to his ankles. "It's back under the bridge for me," he answered. "I've had enough of the crowded corners and tight alleys in the Place Maubert. And I'm tired of sorting rags for that junk dealer. I'm ready for that adventure you're promising me."

Mireli could understand. "That courtyard we rent seems like a cage after the freedom of the long, winding roads," she said, "but the men have found plenty of work for the winter. A city with as many restaurants as Paris has more than enough pots and pans to be mended. Of course the children can talk of nothing but the fields and woods of spring."

"I can't abide children," grumped Armand. "Starlings they are. Witless, twittering, little pests."

Mireli shook her finger at him. "You think you don't like children," she said, "but it is only that you are afraid of them. You're afraid the sly little things will steal your heart if they find out you have one."

Armand grunted and took the handle of the buggy again. Mireli waved him away, swaying on bare feet squeezed into tarnished silver sandals. "If you change your mind about the bridge, you can come to live with us," she invited. "We're beyond the Halles— where they're tearing down the buildings near the old Court of Miracles."

Armand tramped under the black, leafless trees and around the cathedral by the river side without even giving it a glance.

In the green park behind the flying buttresses, some street urchins were loitering. Two of them played at dueling while a third smaller one watched, munching a red apple. The swordsmen, holding out imaginary swords, circled each other. Closer and closer came the clenched fists, then the boys forgot their imaginary swords and began punching each other.

They stopped their play as Armand went by. "Look at the funny old tramp!" one cried to his playmates.

Armand looked around because he wanted to see the funny old tramp too. It must be that droll Louis with his tall black hat and baggy pants. Then he realized that he was the funny old tramp.

"Keep a civil tongue in your head, starling," he ordered. He fingered the holly in his lapel. "If you don't, I'll tell my friend Father Christmas about your rude manners. Then you'll get nothing but a bunch of sticks like these on my buggy."

The boys looked at him with awe. Father Christmas is the Santa Claus of France. He rides down from the north on his little gray donkey and leaves presents for good children.

The small boy held out his half-eaten apple.

"Are you hungry, monsieur?" he asked. "Would you like the rest of this apple?"

But the biggest boy mockingly punched the air with his fist. "Pouf!" he scoffed. "There's no Father Christmas. He's just make-believe."

"If you doubt my word," said Armand with dignity, "just take a look in the Louvre store. You'll find him on the mezzanine floor."

He grinned like one of the roguish gargoyles on the cathedral. There really was a Father Christmas and it was his friend Camille, who felt the urge to work when the weather turned cold.

"I believe you, monsieur," said the boy with the apple. "I saw Father Christmas outside the store yesterday. He was eating hot chestnuts on the street."

Armand hunched his shoulders and quickly walked toward the bridge. Mireli was right. These starlings would steal your heart if you didn't keep it well hidden. And he wanted nothing to do with children. They meant homes and responsibility and regular work—

all the things he had turned his back on so long ago. And he was looking for adventure.

Down a few blocks was the bridge under which he lived when the weather wasn't too raw. And plenty of company he had during the summer with all the homeless of Paris staking their claims to this space or that.

"But first I must have dinner," he told himself, looking up at the restaurant across the street. He licked his thumb and held it up. "The wind is just right," he decided.

So he parked his buggy beside the low wall and settled himself in the breeze that came from the restaurant. He pulled all the kitchen smells deep into his lungs. "Ah, steak broiled over charcoal," he gloated. "And the sauce is just right. But they scorched the potatoes."

For two hours Armand sat on the curb enjoying the food smells because that is the length of time a Frenchman allows himself for lunch in the middle of the day.

Then he daintily wiped his whiskered lips with his cuff and rose to his knobby shoes.

"And just keep the change, waiter," he said generously, although there wasn't a white-uniformed waiter in sight. "You'll need it for Christmas."

He started down the steps that dropped from the street to the quay beside the Seine. He bounced the back wheels of the buggy down each step. "I am really quite stuffed," he told himself, "but I wish I had taken that apple. It would have been the right dessert after such a rich sauce."

Down the quay he pushed the buggy toward the bridge tunnel that ran along the shore. On the cobbled quay a man was washing his car with the free Seine water. A woman in a fur coat was airing her French poodle. A long barge, sleek as a black seal, slid through the river. It was like coming home after a long absence, thought Armand. And anything exciting could happen under a Paris bridge.

As he neared the tunnel, his eyes widened with surprise and anger. A gray canvas was propped over the niche that had always been his own. And a market pushcart was parked by the pillar.

He raced his buggy across the cobblestones toward the arch. When he arrived there, he reached up and angrily tore down the canvas with one swoop of his arm. Then he jumped back in surprise and horror.

"Oh, là, là!" he cried. "Starlings! A nest full of them!"

Because three startled children snuggled into a worn quilt looked up at him with eyes as surprised as his own. The little girl and the boy cowered deeper into the quilt. But the older girl quickly jumped to her feet. She had direct blue eyes and they matched her determined chin and snubbed nose and bright red hair.

"You can't take us away," she cried, clenching her fists. "We're going to stay together because we're a family, and families have to stick together. That's what mama says."

Chapter Two

As Armand glared at the children, a shaggy dog that should have been white came bounding across the quay. It protectively jumped between the tramp and the children, barking fiercely at Armand. The hobo quickly maneuvered his buggy between himself and the dog.

"If that beast bites me," he cried, "I'll sue you for ten thousand francs."

The girl called the dog to her. "Here, Jojo! Come, Jojo! He won't take us away. He's only an old tramp."

The dog stopped barking and sniffed at the wheels of Armand's baby buggy.

The man was insulted. "I'll have you know that I'm not just any old tramp," he said. And

he wasn't. "I'm not friendless, and I could be a workingman right now if I wanted. But where are your parents and who are you hiding from? The police?"

He studied the children closely. Redheads they were, all of them, and their clothes had the mismatched, ill-fitting look of poverty.

The older girl's eyes burned a deep blue. "Our landlady put us out because we don't have enough money to pay for the room since papa died," she explained. "So mama brought us here because we haven't any home now. And she told us to hide behind the canvas so nobody could see us, or they'd take us away from her and put us in a home for poor children. But we're a family, so we want to stay together. I'm Suzy and they're Paul and Evelyne."

The boy swaggered a little. "If I was bigger, I'd find a new place for us to live," he boasted.

"It looks to me like you've already found a new place," said Armand, "and it's my old place. You've put me out of my home just like that landlady did to you."

13

Suzy was apologetic. She moved the push-cart over and measured Armand with one eye closed. Then she carefully drew a long rectangle on the concrete with a piece of soft coal.

"That's your room," she said. "You can live with us." On second thought, she scrawled a small checkered square at the foot of the rectangle. "There's a window," she said gravely, "so you can look out and see the river."

Armand grumbled to himself and pulled his coat tighter across his chest as if to hide his heart. Oh, this starling was a dangerous one. He'd better move on. Paris was full of bridges, the way the Seine meandered through it. No trouble finding another one. But as he started away, the girl ran over and clutched him by his torn sleeve.

"Please stay," she begged. "We'll pretend you're our grandfather."

Armand snorted. "Little one," he said, "next to a millionaire, a grandfather is the last thing I hope to be." But even as he grumbled, he began unpacking his belongings.

He stacked the branches and twigs, and made a pile of the dead leaves he had gathered. He pulled out a dirty canvas and a rusty iron hook. He set a blackened can with a handle near the leaves. He sorted some bent spoons and knives. Last of all, he pulled out an old shoe with a hole in the sole.

"Might come across its mate one of these days," he explained to the children. "And it fits me just right."

The children wanted to help him. Oh, these starlings were clever. They knew how to get around an old man. Lucky he wasn't their grandfather. But he laid his canvas over the rectangle Suzy had made for him.

He started a fire with the branches and dead leaves. Then he hung a big can over the fire. Into it he dropped scraps of food he unwrapped from pieces of newspaper.

"In the good old days of Paris," he told the children, "they used to ring bells in the market places at the close of day so the tramps would know they were welcome to gather up the leftovers. But no more. Nowadays we have to look after ourselves."

They watched him eating his food. Even the dog that should have been white watched each morsel that went into his mouth and drooled on the concrete. Armand wriggled uneasily. "What's the matter?" he asked gruffly. "Haven't you ever seen anybody eat before?" They said nothing in reply, but four pairs of eyes followed each move of his tin spoon. "I suppose you're hungry," he growled. "Starlings always have to be eating. Get your tinware."

Suzy pulled some stained, cracked bowls and twisted spoons from the pushcart. Armand carefully divided the food, even counting in the dog.

It was dark by the time the children's mother joined them. The lights of Paris were floating in the river, but the only light in the tunnel flickered from a tiny fire Armand had made. He could not see the woman's face well, but he felt the edge of her tongue.

"What are you doing here?" she demanded of the hobo.

Armand was angered. "And I might ask you the same, madame," he retorted. "You have taken my piece of the bridge."

"The bridges don't belong to anybody," said the woman. "They're the only free shelter in Paris."

Suzy tried to make peace. "He's a nice, friendly old tramp, mama," she explained, "and he's going to live with us."

"I'm not a friendly old tramp," said Armand indignantly "I'm a mean, cranky old tramp, and I hate children and dogs and women."

"Then if you hate us," said Paul, "why did you give us some of your food?"

"Because I'm a stupid old tramp," replied Armand. "Because I'm a stupid, soft-hearted old tramp." Oh, là, là! There it was. He had let slip that he really had a heart. Now this homeless family would surely be after that too.

The mother was displeased to hear that the children had accepted the hobo's food. "We are not beggars," she reminded them. "I have a steady job at the laundry, and that is more than he can say."

She went to work warming a pan of soup and breaking a long loaf of bread that she had brought with her. Armand sat in the rectangle marked by Suzy and thought that this woman's trouble was pride, and that pride and life under the bridge weren't going to work out well together.

By the dying light of the fire, the woman went back and forth to her pushcart, pulling out moth-eaten blankets and making bed-places on the concrete. Just overhead the automobiles roared, lights garlanded the bridge and people walking along the higher quay laughed lightly. But it could have been a million miles away from the little group under the bridge.

"You ought to put the starlings in some charity home until you find a place of your own, madame," suggested Armand, after the children had dropped off to sleep. "This life is not for them. Now, you wouldn't want them to end up like me, would you?"

"Families should stick together through

19

the lean times as well as the fat," replied the woman. "And I have hopes. I'm going to see my sister-in-law soon. She may know of a place for us out in Clichy."

Armand stretched out on his canvas without bothering about any covering. He was used to the cold. He never felt it any more. But he was sure these children would feel it. As he lay on the hard concrete an uneasy thought worried him, like a mouse gnawing at his shoestring. Now that he had befriended these starlings, his life would never again be completely his own.

When gray morning seeped into the blackness under the bridge, Armand woke to find the woman gone and the three children feeding some stale bread to Jojo.

"Are you still here?" asked Armand. "Don't you go to school or something today?"

Suzy shook her red head. "We can't go to school again until we get a place to live. Mama says the teachers might begin asking us questions, then the people would take us away from her and put us in a home."

"Your mama wants you around more than I do," said Armand. "Children should go to school. Where would I be today if I hadn't gone to school when I was a starling?"

"Oh, I like school," said Suzy with her blue eyes glowing. "I like to read and write. I want to be a teacher when I get big. See, a man on a barge threw this piece of coal to me and I use it for a pencil. I hope we'll soon be able to go back to school again."

"Then that's where we're different," confessed Armand. "I never did like school. But you surely must go some place during the day. Your mama can't expect me to be a nursemaid. I've got places to go."

"Oh, may we go with you?" begged Suzy. "Evelyne is a real good little walker. She won't get tired."

"No," cried Armand in alarm. "You can't go with me, and that's the whole cheese of it."

"Please take us, old tramp," implored Paul. "It's so cold hiding down here with nothing to do."

"That's not polite, Paul," warned Suzy.

21

"Now he won't take us with him unless you apologize."

"But what can I call him?" asked Paul. "I don't know his name."

"What is your name, monsieur?" asked Suzy.

"Armand," replied the hobo.

"But your last name?" asked Paul. "Ours is Calcet."

Armand shrugged his shoulders. "I've forgotten," he admitted. "I think it used to be Pouly or Pougy. Something like that. Just call me Armand."

"All right, Monsieur Armand," said Paul. "I apologize for calling you an old tramp. Now will you take us with you?"

"Of course he will," said Suzy quickly. "He really has a good heart even if he looks so bad. And may Jojo go too?"

Armand clutched at the part of his coat covering his heart. Oh, these starlings were after it, all right. "Oh, là, là!" he exclaimed. "And where would I be seen with three children and a dog?" he demanded. "What friend would want me dropping in with such a company?" Then a sly look crossed his weather-beaten face. Perhaps it wouldn't be a bad idea to take these appealing fledglings out on the street with him. No, indeed! He had a splendid idea. Of course it wasn't just the thing of which that proud mother would approve. "How would you like to go uptown and meet my friend Father Christmas?" he asked the children.

They were so astonished that they couldn't speak for a few seconds. Suzy's eyes grew bluer and bluer with wonder. "Father Christmas!" she finally exclaimed in a hushed voice. "The Father Christmas who brings presents at Christmastime?"

Paul could hardly believe it. "Do *you* know Father Christmas?" he asked.

"Mama said he won't bring us anything this year because he won't be able to find us," said Evelyne.

"Then we're going right up to the Louvre department store," declared Armand, "and tell him where you're living."

Chapter Three

Armand, the Paris hobo, led the redheaded children up the steps to the busy city above. His old mind under his old beret was busy with great plans for the children and himself. Perhaps starlings weren't too bad. They had their uses.

He walked ahead, leading the way across the bridge and around Notre Dame. Suzy followed with Evelyne clinging to her hand. Sometimes Paul lagged to look at something. Sometimes he ran ahead to talk with the hobo. The dog that should have been white trotted along at Suzy's worn-down heels.

They straggled across the bridge that tied

the island to the right bank. The children turned to stare at all the fancy towers and turrets on the roof of the Hôtel de Ville.

"That's the city hall where they run Paris," explained Armand. "Humph! I could run it better from under the bridge."

Blue pigeons fluttered around them hopefully.

"Beggars!" snorted the tramp. "Always pestering folks for a handout." Jojo felt the same way. He chased away any that alighted too close to the children.

"I wish we had some corn to feed them," said Paul.

"See what I mean?" asked Armand. "Even people who haven't any food themselves are ready to feed the pigeons. Wish I was one."

They walked through a dreary, cobbled street until they reached the busy Rue de Rivoli. It was crowded with holiday shoppers.

Christmas was really getting close to the business street. Vendors behind sidewalk stands were bawling out their wares and

imploring passers-by to examine their merchandise. Shoppers were buying earrings and suspenders and water-softeners and silk scarves from the vendors. They were buying frantically and noisily, as if they might never again find anything for sale on the Rue de Rivoli. And the way they were madly buying, perhaps there wouldn't be anything left on the street next day.

Armand was continually having to turn around and coax the children along. They wanted to stop and look at everything. They stopped to stare at a mechanical soldier that a man was demonstrating on the sidewalk. The soldier marched and saluted smartly. It took some time to get Paul away from the soldier.

"Cheap toy," scoffed Armand. "Take it home and it won't work, or the spring will break the first time it's wound. A friend of mine used to sell those things."

No sooner had he coaxed them away from the mechanical toy than they came to a bakery shop. There was a Christmas log cake in the window—such a delicious log. It was chocolatey brown with fancy mushrooms popping from its sweet bark. Pink spun-sugar roses grew out of the chocolate too. And such a real-looking ivy vine twined around it, spreading luscious green leaves.

"Oh, doesn't it look good!" exclaimed Suzy, licking her lips.

"I could eat it all by myself," cried Paul.

"I'm hungry," whined Evelyne.

Armand pulled at each one in turn. "It really tastes like medicine," he said. "All but the vine. That tastes exactly like ivy, tough and bitter. I ate a Christmas log once." The children did not look as if they believed him. "It's a tricky way they have of getting children to take medicine," he insisted.

They crossed the street when the policeman stopped the line of automobiles. They came to a big iron brazier where a man was selling hot chestnuts as fast as he could roast them. The air was warm around the brazier and the smell of chestnuts was tantalizing.

The children stopped and looked hungrily into the brazier.

"Come, come," said Armand impatiently. "Chestnuts are wormy. Do you think Father Christmas is going to wait until midnight for us? We've still got a long way to the Louvre."

But there was so much to see that the way seemed quite short. Soon they were walking through the street arcades of the store building. And it seemed that as much was being sold outside as in—with all the pushcarts and street hawkers.

Armand shepherded his little flock through one of the great glass doors of which the store was so proud. When the children and the dog were once inside, they felt transported into fairyland. It was warm and beautiful in the great store with its bright lights and moving colors. There was an odor of mixed perfumes, as if all the flowers in the world were blooming behind the counters that were covered with soft clothing and glittering jewels.

"We have to go up to the mezzanine," said

Armand. "Might as well use their elevator and save our feet for the walk back."

So they went to the nearest elevator. But all the people waiting could not possibly crowd into it at the same time.

"We'll have to take the steps," decided Armand. "Wouldn't you think some of those women would stay home and do their washing and cooking?"

"Our mother would if she could," said Suzy quickly.

They climbed the stairs. The children's eyes grew dreamier and dreamier. They saw tables piled high with toys. They were entering the domain of Father Christmas. On tiptoe, reverently, they followed the old hobo to the studio where a child could have his picture taken with the saint—providing his parents paid for it.

Armand peeped in. The children stopped breathing.

"He's not here," said the hobo in a disappointed voice.

But even as he spoke, Father Christmas himself came around the counters. He was dressed in a long red robe that reached his ankles, and a curly white beard covered his chest. His mustache was waved and waxed. But his black eyes were snapping as he shook his fist at two boys running ahead of him.

"And if I catch you playing with the electric trains again, I'll put you out of the store," he threatened them.

The Calcet children were frightened. They shrank behind Armand. And as Father Christmas approached them, Evelyne burst into frightened tears and Jojo growled. At sight of Armand, the angry lines left the forehead of Father Christmas and blithely curled around his lips. His eyes softened with pleasure and amusement.

"Ho, ho, ho!" he laughed in the way that Father Christmas should laugh. "Look at whose dear old grandpapa has come to see me today." And he went on with his "ho, ho, ho" until the children were afraid he had a coughing spell.

Armand pulled the little Calcets in front of him, one by one. Evelyne stopped crying and Jojo stopped growling.

"You'd never believe where I found them," said Armand, "but they wanted to come to see you."

The children's eyes were shining again. They were speechless with delight.

"Have you been good children this year?" asked Father Christmas.

"We've tried to be," parried Suzy.

"Sometimes we get mixed up about what's good and what isn't," confessed Paul.

"I pulled Jojo's tail, but I won't do it any more," confessed Evelyne.

Father Christmas was pleased. "I like truthful children," he said. "All the rest of them declare they've been angels all year. Now, what do you want me to bring you for Christmas?"

"We want a house," said Suzy. "Will you please bring us a house, Father Christmas?"

"Ho, ho, ho!" replied Father Christmas.

"That should be agreeable to your parents. And what kind of house do you want? A doll-house?" He glanced down at Jojo. "Or a dog-house?"

"A real house," said Paul. "A house we can live in."

"With walls and a roof," said Suzy.

"And windows," added Evelyne. "I like to watch out of the window when it's time for Suzy and Paul to come home from school."

Father Christmas stopped his jolly "ho, ho, ho" and stared at them. "Who ever heard of children wanting a real house for Christmas?" he asked. "What about a drum for the lad and dolls for you girls?"

"No," insisted Suzy, "it has to be a real house."

Father Christmas rolled his black eyes around and twirled the ends of his mustache. "It will have to be dolls or games," he said. "My little donkey can't carry a house on his back. You know that."

The children's faces fell. Then Suzy

remembered her manners. "Thank you anyway, Father Christmas," she said in a quivering voice. "I guess we don't want anything
but a house."

"I do," said Paul. "I want something to
eat."

"And I want a doll," added Evelyne.

Father Christmas started to speak, but a
pretty salesgirl interrupted him. "You better
get into the studio or Monsieur Latour will fire
you," she said. "There are four children waiting to have their pictures taken."

Father Christmas patted each red head in
farewell. Then he said to Armand, "Our
Monsieur Latour is looking for a night watchman for a friend's building. Want the job?"

"Oh, là, là!" exclaimed Armand. "I didn't
come here to ask Father Christmas for a job.
Good-by, Camille."

He led the children down the steps again,
but now they were strangely silent. Even
Jojo's ears drooped and his tail dragged.

The main floor was less crowded as they

walked between the counters. An elegant floorwalker caught sight of the vagabonds. He hurried to them. He made a little noise as he tapped the immaculately white handkerchief peeping from his breast pocket.

"Aren't you in the wrong store?" he asked haughtily.

"I should say we're in the wrong store," replied Armand, just as haughtily. "We brought our dog in here to ride the escalators, and all I see is those crowded elevators." He whistled to Jojo. "Come, boy, we'll take you over to the Printemps."

Jojo growled at the haughty floorwalker. The little group headed for the great glass door of which the store was so proud. They shivered as they stepped out in the cold, biting air.

Chapter Four

"There's a fancy Christmas window out here you should see," said Armand to the children. He wanted to cheer them because they were so silent and forlorn.

He led them to the main doors facing the Palais Royal square. A crowd of people blocked the window, but the tramp and his companions wormed their way to the front.

The children's eyes bulged. Such a grand sight they had never seen. A scroll near the front of the window said that the scene was "The Marriage of Tartine." It was truly a wedding out of a storybook. Two mechanical figures, a man and a woman dressed in gorgeous white costumes of long ago, stood in a high pavilion. They bowed sedately to each other while music tinkled romantically. But even more remarkable was the parade of tiny figures below the lovers. They were white-capped cooks bearing wondrous dishes to the wedding feast. One carried a gaudy peacock which raised and lowered its neck in time to the tune. Another held up a great crab that clicked out the rhythm with its claws. And yet another carried a cake even fancier than the Christmas log in the bakery window. Each little cook was so proud of his dish that he waltzed around and around as he paraded.

"I bet they will live in a beautiful castle after the wedding," sighed Suzy, gazing at the lovely bride and groom.

"I'm hungry," said Paul.

"Me, too," agreed Evelyne.

The dog that should have been white was drooling on a man's shoes.

A crafty look came into Armand's eyes.

"I bet you know the words of that tune

they're playing," he coaxed. "It's 'Dame
Tartine.' If you'll sing it for me, I'll get you
something to eat."

Paul put his hand over his mouth. Evelyne
put her finger in hers. Suzy shyly shook her
head. "There are too many people here," she
said.

"Then sing for them," said Armand.
"Don't be stupid starlings without a song in
your throats. Open your little beaks and sing
like canaries."

So Paul pulled his hand from his mouth
and began to sing in a thin but firm voice.
Then Suzy joined him in a sweet, high tone.
Evelyne took her finger out of her mouth and
chirped with them. They sang like three little
birds on a branch in the springtime.

When they had finished two verses,
Armand clapped hard. Then he pulled his beret
off his head and held it out to one person after
another in the crowd.

"Alms," he begged. "Alms for a poor old

grandfather with three fatherless children to clothe and feed. And an orphan dog."

The people gave generously because they felt the spirit of Christmas. The coins clinked into the hobo's beret.

The concert had been so successful that Armand waited until the first audience left and a new one came to look at the window. Then he had the children sing again. And again he passed his beret for coins.

This might have gone on for some time if the haughty floorwalker hadn't come out of the store to see why the crowd around the window was bigger than ever. He scowled at the quartet.

"On your way," he ordered them with a wave of his hand and his nose in the air. "No begging in front of the Louvre."

Armand did not mind leaving. His beret was heavy with francs, which he funneled into his pocket.

"Come, canaries," he said. "You are good children. I'll treat you to pancakes."

He took them around the corner to where

a Breton man stood behind a stand making thin pancakes on two round black irons.

"I'll take a dozen for a starter," ordered Armand, but he had to show his money before the Breton would pour the batter on an iron.

One by one the man made the pancakes, so slowly that the children thought they would die of hunger before he had made a full dozen. The smell was even better than that of the perfume in the Louvre. The cakes were big as scooter wheels and thin as silk. The Breton spread each one with butter and jelly, then folded it twice. Everyone got three pancakes. Then Jojo whined pitifully and they remembered that he was probably hungry too. So Armand ordered another dozen pancakes.

They started back, munching happily on their pancakes, but Jojo kept on whining because he had swallowed each of his in one big gulp.

When they reached a corner where a crowd of shoppers was waiting for buses, Armand suggested to the children that they entertain the weary people with some Christmas carols. The little Calcets were less shy this time. They sang as loud as they could.

As before, the hobo passed his beret around. "Alms," he begged, "so a poor old man can feed his starving children."

But as the coins fell into his cap, an angry fist rapped against his back. Armand was frightened because he thought it was a policeman. But it was only another man as ragged as himself. A big box hung from his neck, and in it a little monkey dressed in a red-and-green suit made faces through a screen.

"What do you mean cutting into my territory?" demanded the man with the monkey. "You're stealing my show."

Armand tried to make peace. "Now, don't let's cross swords, Titi," he said. "There's enough of a crowd for both of us. The kind of people who like to listen to choirs wouldn't be interested in watching a monkey make faces anyway."

Titi was not soothed. "Children or monkeys, what's the difference?" he demanded. "And this is my corner."

But the children did not join in the quarrel, although Jojo barked at the monkey and the monkey made his worst face at the dog. Then the monkey gave the children a sad smile and held out its green cap to them.

"Oh, he wants money too," said Suzy, "and there's a bowl on top of the box for coins. Please give the little monkey some money, Monsieur Armand."

"Indeed I will not," snapped Armand.

"Please, please, monsieur," begged Evelyne. "The little monkey wants to buy some pancakes too."

By this time most of the shoppers had boarded their buses. Armand tried to hustle his choir away, but the children wouldn't let him leave until he had dropped a coin in the bowl for the monkey.

"That Titi is a fake," explained the hobo as they walked down the street. "He's just using the monkey to make money for himself." And he rattled the coins in his own pocket.

When they came to the chestnut vendor, he treated them again. They waited as long as they could before eating the chestnuts because the hot shells warmed their hands.

"Now, remember," Armand cautioned the children, "not a word about this to your mama and I'll take you with me every day."

But when Madame Calcet came wearily down the steps that evening, the children rushed to meet her.

"I saved a pancake for you, mama," cried Suzy, digging into the pocket of her faded coat. "It's cold now, but it still tastes sweet."

Paul reached into his coat pocket too. "And I brought you some chestnuts, mama," he said. "They're cold too, but they'll taste good."

Evelyne began to sob. "I didn't save anything for you, mama," she wept. "I forgot."

Madame Calcet hugged her. "Never mind," she said, "I've brought something for you."

Then her voice grew suspicious. "Where did you get the pancake and the chestnuts?" she asked.

Suzy and Paul lowered their eyes.

"We sang songs, and people dropped money in Monsieur Armand's cap," said Evelyne.

Madame Calcet flung the children's gifts to the ground. She angrily advanced toward the hobo, who was stretched out on his canvas. "You've turned my children into beggars," she accused. "You've been using them for begging on the streets."

"Now, now, madame." Armand tried to quiet her. "When the grand singers at the Opera get paid for their songs, is that begging? I'll give you your share."

But Madame Calcet was busy tearing down canvases and gathering up blankets. "I don't want any of your ill-gotten money," she retorted. "We are going to leave here," she cried to the children. "I forbid you to have anything more to do with him."

The children began to wail. Even Jojo howled dismally because he seemed to sense that there wouldn't be any more pancakes on the Rue de Rivoli.

Armand proudly rose to his knobby shoes. "No need, madame," he said as haughtily as he had spoken to the floorwalker. "I'll leave myself and save you the trouble. I know when I'm not welcome."

It took him very little time to pack his baby buggy.

"Don't go," cried Suzy. "Please don't let him go, mama."

"He's our grandpa," sobbed Evelyne.

"He's all we have but you," added Paul.

But Armand thrust out his bearded chin. "You just keep your old bridge, madame," he said. "It'll be a long time until you find anything else. Good-by, starlings!"

Then he bumped his buggy down the quay. He clattered it as noisily as he could so it would drown out the sound of the children's laments and the dog's howling.

Chapter Five

Armand scowled ferociously as he pushed his buggy along the river. He walked through another bridge tunnel. It was deep and inviting and there were iron rings over which he could hang his things. But the Paris fireboats were moored along the quay.

"Comes a fire on the waterfront and all of Paris will gather on my roof," he mumbled.

So he plodded on to another bridge. He only stopped once to watch a man pull in his fishing line because he thought there was a big fish on the hook. But it was only a sodden shoe.

"Ah, that's the way our hopes go, monsieur," Armand sadly told the fisherman. Then he began jumping up and down with excitement. "The mate to the one in my buggy," he cried. "That's it!"

The fisherman yanked the old shoe off the hook and tossed it to Armand. "Oh, là, là, monsieur," said the hobo, "but that just goes to show we should never give up hope."

At last he found a bridge shelter that suited him. He spread his canvas as carefully as a family man laying the rug in a new house.

"This isn't as cozy as the room that canary made for me," he admitted. "Funny how those black lines on the concrete kept out the draft."

And he didn't sleep well that night. He kept wondering about the children. Were they warm enough? Wouldn't they be lonely? He tried to pretend to himself that he was fretting about something else. "It was my bridge," he said aloud. "They had no right to put me off my own property. I ought to go back and assert my rights."

50

When he woke up next morning, he noticed that a light snow had fallen during the night. He sat up and rubbed his eyes as he looked out at the quay. Paris had turned white overnight. It was a beautiful sight for those who could stand in a warm room and look through a window. What would the children do now? They'd probably play in it and get their death of cold with no grownup to look after them.

"I'll show them," growled Armand. "I'm going right back there and tell them what's what. I'd like to see them try to put me off my own property again."

So back he trundled his buggy, and the wheels left wet black lines in the snow. There was no sign of life around the fireboats. But as he neared the old bridge tunnel, two women in fur coats came walking down the quay. In alarm Armand noticed that the trail they were leaving behind them ended at the canvas propped against the wall. He quickened his shuffling steps. As the two women passed, they turned their heads toward him.

"Poor, wretched creature!" exclaimed the woman in the black fur coat.

"Perhaps we could save him," said the woman in the brown fur coat.

"Oh, go feed the pigeons," jeered Armand.

His big footprints erased theirs in the melting snow. He pulled the canvas aside. The children were crying.

"What's the matter?" asked Armand. "You still bawling because I left? You might have known I'd come back."

Suzy pulled Evelyne closer. "Two women were here talking to us," she sobbed. "They've gone to get somebody."

"They're going to take us away and put us some place," said Paul, wiping his eyes.

"And they say they're going to put mama in jail," Suzy wept. "Oh, please help us, Monsieur Armand. Please don't stay mad at mama."

Armand kept twisting his beret around on his gray head. Now the soup was spilled into the fire. He knew women like those two in the fur coats. Always trying to make hoboes go to

52

work or wash their faces or read books. And now they were picking on children. Must have run out of hoboes. It really wasn't his affair, but Mireli had been right. These little ones— He pulled his beret down tightly. That was it. Mireli!

"Start packing your loot in your cart," he ordered. "We've got to get out of here fast. Women like those two don't give up easy when they have a mind to save poor wretches."

He helped the children gather together the few pans and fold the blankets. He pulled down the canvas and covered the cart with it.

"But where will we go?" asked Suzy.

"Mama won't know where we are," cried Paul. "We can't leave mama. She's the most of our family."

"I'll come back and tell your mama where you are," said Armand. "I've got just the right nest for you."

He had to help them get their market cart up the steps. Then because Evelyne's feet were so cold, he sat her in his buggy on top of his possessions. He pushed her down the street and across the bridges. Suzy and Paul followed, pushing the cart.

"If I were a big man," said Paul, "I wouldn't let those women be so bossy."

"Where are we going?" asked Suzy as they came to the Rue de Rivoli. "To get Father Christmas to help us?"

Armand looked back. "You don't need Father Christmas to help you," he said. "You've got me. Besides, he's too busy. It's only four days until Christmas."

"Will you tell him we've left the bridge?" asked Suzy anxiously. "Just in case he does find a way to bring us a house?"

"Now, don't you worry," said Armand. "Leave everything to me."

Instead of leading them down the Rue de Rivoli, he waited for the automobiles to stop. He motioned the children to come alongside him with their pushcart. They crossed the street abreast, and just as they reached the curb a taxicab splashed them with dirty slush. But they kept on, single file again.

Ahead of them loomed a giant shed. It was as big as a railroad station and as black and noisy.

"The Halles," Armand called back to them. "That's the big central market where all the food comes into Paris."

The children quickened their steps at the word "food."

"I'm hungry," said Paul.

"Well, you needn't get hungry at the Halles," replied the hobo. "They sell most of the stuff wholesale. But a fellow like me can sometimes wangle some food there. I'll try my luck."

They saw that whole streets were covered by black sheds. Now they had to pick their way carefully. The sidewalks were cluttered with crates and baskets. The pavement was slimy with torn red, white and blue papers.

They kept bumping into things because they were so busy goggling at the sights. Boxes of fruit and vegetables made walls around them. There were long alleys with endless rows of beef, sheep and hog carcasses hanging on hooks. Men went by carrying great baskets filled with hocks and pigs' feet and calves' heads.

A man was lifting an immense box. He wore an outlandish hat which made him look like a carnival figure.

"Who is he?" asked Suzy, pointing. "Why does he wear that funny hat?"

"He's one of the strong ones," answered Armand. "He's mighty proud of that hat because wearing it means he can carry four hundred and forty pounds at one time."

"Can you?" asked Paul.

Armand shuddered. "Oh, là, là! I'll never know," he declared.

They hurried past trucks backed to the curb, and lines of desks where buyers and sellers did their business.

As they came out into the street behind the Halles, Armand met many old friends. Ragged men and women were picking through the old vegetables and fruit thrown into the gutter.

"Hello, Charlot." He waved to a bleary-eyed man with his clothing held together by safety pins. "Good morning, Marguerite," he greeted a woman dressed in men's clothes. "Found any diamonds in the trash cans?"

Then he bumped into a six-wheeled metal cart pushed by a man with a tall hat and baggy pants. "Well, if it isn't Louis," he exclaimed. "Making enough money to pay your rent in that mole tunnel off the Place Maubert?"

Louis grinned toothlessly. "I can get you a job today," he offered. "They need more pushers. They always do."

Armand started away. "I'm pushing," he said. "And you can see I've got my own pushers with me. So long."

The children hated to leave the Halles. They had enjoyed the noise and bustle.

"And with all that food," said Suzy, "wouldn't you think they could spare us just a little bit?"

They pushed their carts past St. Eustache church and into a street teeming with other carts. It was as if the great market had spilled into this street in streams of fish and meat stands along both curbs.

Paul stopped to look in the window of a coffee shop where colorful stuffed birds of South America were posed on open bags of coffee beans.

The asphalt pavement ended when the Rue de Montorgueil became the Rue des Petits Carreaux. Now they tramped over patterns of cobbles so tiny that they looked like mosaic.

Armand stopped them when they came to a building with three black Egyptian heads trimming its front. He pointed to a narrow, winding alleyway.

"Part of the old Court of Miracles," he said. "In the early days of Paris, all the beggars gathered back in there for shelter, and nobody dared bother them."

He led them into the ancient alley with its dingy shops.

"Why did they call it the Court of Miracles?" asked Suzy.

"Because it was like miracles the way those fake beggars shed their crutches and bandages when they came back here at night," explained Armand. "Then they'd feast and make merry. Even had their own king they elected."

The children looked disappointed to see the rear of a great garage and some more dark stores taking the place of the old court of the beggars.

"I bet you'd be the king if they still lived here," said Paul.

Armand sighed. "Oh, là, là! Those were the good old days," he said, as if he had lived in them himself and were remembering.

They left the court with its rakish memories. They passed the doorways of dilapidated roominghouses. In each they could dimly see a battered old stairway, barely wide enough for a child, curving up to dark halls above or perhaps a magic tower room—who knew?

Looking up at a high window across the street, they saw a queer old lady hanging out her washing on lines stretched across the window. And her washing was six long red pairs of underpants and six long red gloves, as if she might have been the wife of Father Christmas.

At last they came to an open corner fenced in by wooden boards. Above it rose the crags of buildings which were slowly being torn down, floor by floor. Only the tall, jagged walls were left standing, like rocky mountain peaks. On some of them one could trace the original rooms by the great squares of faded wallpaper.

They could hear a clattering and banging behind the fence as if the workmen were busy at their destruction. But when Armand guided them through an opening, the children's eyes opened wide.

The sandy yard was filled with makeshift tents. Two rattle-trap automobiles were parked among them. Dark-skinned men gathered around a fire were beating on old pans with hammers. There were black-eyed women with gaudy skirts dragging over the wet sand. Children with half-wild fox faces stared at them. Then five dogs came bounding toward them, snarling and barking.

Before they knew what had happened, Jojo sprang at the dogs. There was a flying, barking mass of fur and growls. Then a gypsy woman came running with a stick. She began beating the snarling dogs without playing favorites. They stopped fighting and howled in pain and fright. Armand grabbed Jojo and pulled him back. The gypsy woman dropped the stick and began talking to the dogs in a low, soft voice. They whined a little, then sniffed at Jojo in a friendly way, as if he had now been properly introduced.

"Armand," cried Mireli. "Welcome, old friend. You look as if you have come to stay for a while." She looked at the children. Paul and Suzy were peeping fearfully around the tramp's back. "Welcome, little ones," she said. "You will not be lonely here. I will get you something to eat." She helped Evelyne down from the buggy.

"We don't come emptyhanded," said Armand. He began pulling things out of his buggy. First, a bunch of celery. Next, a couple of apples. Lastly, he proudly held up a dressed calf's head.

He saw the little Calcets staring at the food as surprised as if he were a magician who had lifted it from a hat. "Don't know how that stuff dropped into my buggy," he said to them. "Specially with Evelyne on top. I must have brushed against something in the Halles."

The gypsy children closed in on the little Calcets. The boys were coatless and wore patched pantaloons. The little girls were dressed in gaudy skirts that hung to the ground from under their torn coats. Their long black hair was cut in bangs over their beady eyes. But they thought the Calcets were the odd-looking ones. They fingered Evelyne's red hair. They felt Suzy's dark, rough coat, then touched their own gay rags.

"Your clothes look so sad," said a gypsy girl, "but you have happy hair."

A gypsy man put down his hammer and greeted them as warmly as Mireli. "There is always room for one or ten more in our camp," he said. "You can share the tent with Petro, Armand. He is in bed there now. He doesn't like the cold, so he sleeps all winter."

"Can the girls live in the van with us?" cried a gypsy girl about Suzy's age. Her clothes were the brightest of all and she wore golden rings in her ears, but her high shoes clomped like boots because they had no laces.

"And you can live in our tent," a tall boy offered Paul. "It's near a bakery wall, so it's nice and warm."

The gypsy girl took Suzy by the hand. "My name's Tinka," she said. "What is yours?"

"Tinka," repeated Suzy. "What a beautiful name! I'm Suzy Calcet, and this is my brother, Paul, and my little sister, Evelyne. We don't have a home anywhere."

"I'll show you our home," Tinka offered.

"I'll show Paul and Evelyne too." She led the Calcets through an alley of tents. In the far corner was Tinka's home. The redheaded Calcets gasped at sight of it. It was a tiny house with a domed roof and carved brown doors and shutters. Instead of sitting on the ground, it was perched on wheels.

"A gypsy house on wheels," said Paul. "Now, that's the kind of home I'd like to have."

"We can take our house anywhere we want," said Tinka proudly. "We just hook it to the back of Uncle Nikki's automobile."

Suzy's eyes began to burn like blue flames. She squeezed Paul's arm. "Father Christmas' little donkey could bring us a house on wheels," she cried. "He could pull it."

"Let's tell Monsieur Armand," said Paul. "Then he can tell Father Christmas what we've decided."

Chapter Six

The children's desire for a house on wheels worried Armand. Now, wouldn't it take them to think up something like that?

"You don't need to have Father Christmas bring you a house now," he said. "Tinka will let you live in that one with her. And Paul will be in a comfortable tent."

"But we want our own house," said Suzy. "A house for our own family to live in. Then we can take the wheels off so we can stay in one place."

"No, let's leave the wheels on," cried Paul. "Let's keep moving to new places. I'd like to live like a gypsy."

"But if you move all the time, you won't be able to go to school," Suzy reminded him.

Paul looked as if that was not worrying him.

The inside of the house on wheels was as nice as the outside. A big featherbed filled the back of it. There were shelves running all along the walls, and brightly scrubbed copper pans hung over the tiny stove. Suzy could see that the little house was the tidiest place in the gypsy camp.

"We put more featherbeds on the floor at night so we can all sleep here," explained Tinka. "All the girls. But we can't muss anything because mother keeps a neat house."

They stayed in the house on wheels for a long time. Tinka squatted on the floor and told them stories of her travels.

"Every spring we go way down to Provence on the Mediterranean Sea," she said. "We camp among old Roman ruins and bathe in the warm streams. Will you come to Provence with us?"

Suzy was tempted, but she shook her head stubbornly. "I have to go to school," she said. "I don't think mama would go anyway. And we couldn't go without her. We're a family and we have to stick together."

Tinka understood. "We gypsies stick together too," she said.

The time went so fast that Armand had almost forgotten about the children's mother.

"You wait here and I'll go fetch her," he said as he noticed that it was almost dark.

He hurried back through the streets, where the snow had turned into water. The Halles were noisier and busier than ever because most of the work there took place during the night when the great trucks rolled in from all over France, bringing food to hungry Paris.

It was dark by the time he reached the bridge. He caught Madame Calcet just in time. She was already descending the steps.

At first she wouldn't even listen to him. She hastened down without turning her head.

But when she saw that her children and all their belongings were gone, she was only too willing to listen. She burst into tears when Armand told her about the two women.

"Why can't they leave me in peace with my children?" she said. "I'm only trying to keep my family together."

"It's all right, madame," said Armand, patting her shoulder. "The nestlings are safe with some good friends of mine. And you will be welcome there too. I should have thought of it before. It's so much better than under the bridge."

Madame Calcet stopped crying and followed him back toward the Halles.

"I want to apologize to you," she said humbly. "You are a good man."

Armand felt uncomfortable. "Wait until you meet my friends," he said. He was certain that she would not thank him when she saw them.

All the way through the dimly lit streets, Madame Calcet followed several steps behind him. Armand knew it was because she was ashamed to be seen with a hobo. But he did not let that bother him. He had lost his pride long ago.

Work at the Halles had reached a fever peak the third time he went through it. Now the woman had to stay close to him so that she would not get lost. They were pushed by baskets, and once Madame Calcet was almost run over by a truck. It was a relief to get back into the dark alleys.

But when Armand led his companion through the wooden fence, the woman acted in the way he had expected. Her eyes flashed wide at the sight before them.

The dusky gypsies were gathered around a campfire. The building peaks rising behind them made the scene one of a lonely gypsy camp at the foot of a bare Spanish mountain instead of in the crowded heart of Paris.

One of the men was playing a guitar and a girl was dancing. Behind her pranced Tinka, trying to learn the steps by heart. And the firelight fell on three redheaded children clapping their hands in time to the music.

"Gypsies!" shrieked Madame Calcet. "You have brought us to *gypsies!*" Then, in her shame and despair, she started sobbing bitterly into her twisted scarf.

"Madame," said Armand, "you cry so much that you will bring down the rain."

"To think we have fallen so low," wept the woman. "My children at home with gypsies."

"What is wrong with gypsies?" asked Armand. "Why do you think you are better? Are you kinder? Are you more generous?"

"I'm honest," murmured the woman through her scarf.

"What good does it do to be honest if you aren't kind and generous?" he asked. Then in a softer tone he said, "You may think them thieves and wanderers, madame, but they are workers too. They are proud of their fine metalwork, and they have a right to be. They are expert craftsmen. Can you mend a pan that has half of the bottom burned out?"

"They are thieves," persisted Madame Calcet.

"They mean no harm," said the hobo. "They don't know there's a commandment against stealing. And you've been doing a lot of talking about families sticking together. Well, we're all God's big poor family, so we need to stick together and help each other."

Madame Calcet began drying her eyes on her scarf. "I have nowhere else to take the children," she admitted. "The room my sister-in-law told me about is more than I can pay. I must be grateful for shelter, I guess."

The gypsies received her courteously, and Mireli even offered to tell her fortune, although Madame Calcet refused. Tinka brought her a bowl of stew to eat by the fireside. "It's good pigeon stew," she explained. "My Uncle Nikki catches them in the square. He has very swift hands."

Madame Calcet looked distastefully at the stew, but hunger triumphed. "It is really very good," she admitted after the first spoonful.

The three children gathered around their mother's skirts.

"It is so much nicer here than under the bridge," said Paul.

"And you must see the darling little house on wheels," cried Suzy. "Monsieur Armand is going to tell Father Christmas to bring us one."

"You may sleep in it," Mireli politely told Madame Calcet. "There is a soft bed for you and your girls in the back."

"You are very kind," said Madame Calcet. "But I expect to pay you for our stay here."

"We do not take money from our friends," said Mireli proudly. "Only from strangers." Then she disappeared behind a tent.

Suzy found it more fun to sleep on a featherbed on the floor with the gypsy children.

Early the next morning Madame Calcet returned to her job. Later the gypsy men left to canvas the restaurants for more pots and pans to mend.

"I guess you are having your Christmas

vacation from school now," Suzy said to Tinka, since the children remained in the courtyard.

"We have vacation all the time," said Tinka. "We don't go to school."

Suzy was shocked. "Then how do you learn to read and write?" she asked.

"We don't know how to read or write," said Tinka.

Suzy was even more shocked. "Then I will teach you," she said. "We will have school this morning."

She brought out her well-rubbed piece of coal. She had plenty of blank walls to use for a blackboard. She carefully printed each letter of the alphabet, naming it as she wrote.

Armand was stretched out on the ground with a piece of firewood for a pillow. He was watching the little schoolteacher with good humor. "You the one who's been writing all those signs on walls and posts telling folks to go home?" he asked.

Suzy gravely shook her head. Then she

held the coal out to Tinka. "Now you copy them," she ordered.

Tinka gave her a foxlike grin. Below Suzy's letters she quickly drew two circles, one inside the other.

Suzy frowned. "That isn't a letter. It doesn't mean anything."

"Oh, yes it does," said Tinka, grinning. "If you see that sign near a gate, it means that the people who live inside are good and generous." She quickly scratched an upright line, then crossed it with two short bars. "But that sign means that beggars will be badly received. Perhaps the people will even set the dog on them."

Armand came to life. "I'll remember that," he said. "Seems like I went to the wrong school. Never learned such useful reading."

Tinka laughed. She mischievously batted her eyelashes at Suzy. "See," she said, "there is some writing *you* can't read."

Suzy was willing to be a pupil as well as a teacher. "I like to learn new things," she told

Tinka. "Now you teach me some more gypsy writing."

Armand stiffly rose to his feet. "It's getting too highbrow for me around here," he said. "Think I'll take a little walk over town."

This time the children did not plead to be taken along. They were no longer bored and lonely. Although Paul and the boys had quickly lost interest in Suzy's school, they were all playing a game of wolf-and-sheep between the tents.

But Suzy had one request. "Will you please go to the Louvre store, Monsieur Armand," she asked, "and tell Father Christmas where to bring our house? And that we'll be satisfied if he brings us a little one on wheels like Tinka's?"

Armand nodded. "That's right," he remembered. "Not much time left. Tomorrow night is Christmas Eve."

Chapter Seven

The day before Christmas, the little Calcets could talk about nothing but the house on wheels which they expected Father Christmas to bring them. Even the gypsy children were excited about it.

"Then you'll surely come to Provence with us in the spring," tempted Tinka. "Petro's car can pull your house. We'll all make the pilgrimage to the shrine of Saint Sara."

"Who is Saint Sara?" asked Suzy. "I never heard of her."

Tinka was amazed. "If you went to school," she said, "I should think you would have learned more. Don't you know that after the Crucifixion, Saint Mary Jacobe and Saint Mary Salome were seized by the enemies of Christ and set adrift in a boat without any rudder or sails? And of course Saint Sara was with them because she was their handmaiden. The wind blew their boat to the shores of Provence. So now there's a church there and Saint Sara's statue is in the crypt. The gypsies make a pilgrimage there in May because Saint Sara was a gypsy."

"I want to see Saint Sara," said Evelyne.

"I want to see the Mediterranean Sea," said Paul.

"I would like to see all of those things too," said Suzy wistfully, "but we will have to finish our school first."

"We can't go to school until we get a home," Paul reminded her. "Remember what mama said?"

"But we'll have a home when school starts," said Suzy.

"Father Christmas is going to bring our house tonight."

Armand groaned. If only he could get them off the house idea.

"How would you like to go to a Christmas Eve party tonight?" he asked. "A big party with food and singing and hundreds of people?"

As he had expected, the Calcets immediately forgot their house on wheels.

"Where?" asked Paul. "In a big palace?"

"Not exactly," replied Armand. "It's to be held under the Tournelle Bridge." Paul's face fell. "But it will be a grand party, I can promise you," went on Armand. "The Notre Dame church people give it every Christmas Eve for all the hoboes of Paris and their ladies. They'll sing carols and eat sauerkraut and wieners."

Paul was happy again. "I like to eat," he said, "and I like to eat sauerkraut and wieners best of all."

"Maybe mama won't let us go," said Suzy.

"She can go too," said Armand. "After all, it's for homeless people, so that makes her a distinguished guest."

80

"Can the gypsies go too?" asked Suzy. "I'd like to take Tinka."

But the gypsies said they had their own plans for Christmas Eve. Tinka only grinned and acted secretive when she was questioned about them.

Strangely enough, Madame Calcet agreed to go to the holiday party under the bridge. "I can do so little for the children this year," she said. "And they have some crazy idea that Father Christmas is going to bring them a gypsy van. Perhaps the party will make them forget."

But even though the gypsies refused to go to the party, Nikki offered to drive them there in his rattletrap car.

"I've some business in the Jardin des Plantes park and have to take the car out anyway," he explained.

The Calcets were thrilled. They had never ridden in an automobile. They clung tightly to the seats. Jojo sat erect as if he were quite used to it.

81

Nikki raced down the narrow streets and shouted insults at pedestrians and cars that got in his way. His own car sputtered, rattled and clanked as if it would fall apart any moment. But it didn't.

It was a cold, clear night and all the monuments were floodlighted. The streetlights threw golden ribbons across the Seine. The old car rattled across the Tournelle Bridge, then stopped at the curb. The Calcets jumped out quickly. Armand stiffly backed out. Jojo made it in one leap.

From the head of the steps they could look down on the party. As Armand had predicted, it was crowded. A large tent had been raised on the quay—a tent that would have delighted the gypsies. Young boys and girls of the parish were carrying out pans of steaming food from the tent. The warm smell of sauerkraut was overpowering. It delighted Paul most of all.

"Let's hurry down before they eat it all up," he urged.

But Suzy's eyes were looking across the river to the little Isle of the Cité, where Notre Dame was illuminated like a saint's dream. Its flying buttresses and tall, fragile arrow were frosted with light.

"Isn't it beautiful?" sighed Suzy. "It looks like it was made in a bakery shop, doesn't it?"

But Madame Calcet had turned around to look up at the fashionable restaurant rising over the bridge, a man-made cliff honey-combed with lights.

"There are rich people in beautiful clothes sitting at white tables up there," she said enviously.

"And paying a lot of money for rich food that's going to give them indigestion," said Armand. "Come on! That sauerkraut smells like a feast to me."

When they reached the bottom of the steps, they could see that the tunnel was even more crowded than the quay. Canvas had been stretched across the far end to cut off the draft. There were colored ribbons fastened to it. A decorated tree stood on a high stage made of boards. Charcoal heaters had been set around to warm the air, and many of the ragged guests were huddled over them. Others sat on the curb greedily eating out of tin bowls. And some lady hoboes were sitting with their backs against the bridge, talking about politics and trash cans and chilblains. But most of the hoboes only stood around waiting for something to happen.

Armand cornered a young girl carrying some tin bowls. "Right here!" he said. "This is where we said we'd be waiting for you."

He made room for the Calcets to sit along the curb, but Madame Calcet remained standing.

"I'll help you carry out the food," she offered the girl. "I'm not really a tramp."

Besides sauerkraut and wieners, there was soup, pork, cheese and oranges. Armand ate until he felt as if he would burst. They took turns feeding tidbits to Jojo. "Have to store up like the camel for next Christmas Eve," Armand told the children.

They needed no urging. But Suzy kept asking, "When are we going back?"

"Don't you like the party?" asked Armand. "Look! There's a man on the stage who's going to play the accordion so we can all sing carols. You don't want to go now, do you?"

"Not really," said Suzy. "It's just that I can't wait to see if Father Christmas brought us the gypsy house."

Armand stopped gnawing on a wiener. There it was again. Now the nestlings would go back to the courtyard only to be bitterly disappointed. He couldn't bear the thought of spoiling this wonderful night with its free food and entertainment. He lowered his voice.

"Listen," he said to the children. "Father Christmas made me promise not to tell this, but there isn't going to be any house on wheels for you. Too many gypsy children asked for them this year, so he didn't have any left over."

"No home for us?" asked Suzy in a quivering voice. The flickering light from the charcoal burners made the tears in her eyes sparkle like diamonds. "You mean he's not going to give us *any* kind of a house?"

"I don't mean that at all," parried Armand. "Oh, I'm not supposed to tell you this, but the truth of it is he's having a house built for you out in Neuilly. And it isn't finished yet. You don't build a house during a few Christmas holidays, you know. It takes some time. They haven't even got the plumbing in yet."

Suzy's eyes shone brighter than diamonds. "A real house?" she asked in a hushed voice. "A house growing out of the ground?"

Armand nodded. "But not a word to your mama," he said. "Remember that. I shouldn't even have told you. I gave Father Christmas my solemn promise that I would keep it a secret."

But the children were kept too busy to tell their mother. And Madame Calcet was kept quite busy herself because more hoboes had come to the party than had been expected. But it is easy to stretch sauerkraut and wieners.

Then the crowd of hoboes and their ladies and friends sang Christmas carols to the accordion music. Most of their voices were cracked and off key, but they sounded beautiful to themselves.

Armand was ready to go by midnight. He clung to the big carton that had been given him at the tent as a gift. He knew it was full of jam, fruit and cigarettes. It would be his Christmas present to the gypsies.

But Madame Calcet wouldn't think of going straight back. "We must go to the midnight mass on the quay," she said. "The girl told me about it."

An altar had been set up on the Tournelle quay right out in the open. The priest in his bright vestments, followed by his altar boys, had just approached the altar by the time Armand and the Calcets arrived. Many of the hoboes stayed for the mass.

Evelyne fell asleep in her mother's arms. Jojo was quiet and respectful although it was the first time he had ever been to church.

Armand swayed from one foot to the other uneasily. It had been so long since he had gone to mass. Lucky this one was out here on the quay. They never would have pulled him into one of those great fancy churches.

The hobo had other things to make him uneasy. The plight of this family. Just how had he got himself so tied up with them? How had he blundered into such a trap? It was the way those starlings had begged him to stay with them. That is how they had stolen his heart. No one had ever made him feel needed before. And now he'd lied to them. There wasn't any house growing out of the ground— not for them.

In his misery he raised his eyes high over the altar—up to the stars in the Paris sky. "Please, God," he said, moving his lips soundlessly, "I've forgotten how to pray. All I know now is how to beg. So I'm begging you to find a roof for this homeless family."

Then he was ashamed to notice that he was

holding his beret up in his usual begging way. He quickly pulled it over his head.

When they got back to the camp in the early morning hours, they found all the gypsies awake, even Petro. They soon learned why.

"Look!" cried Tinka with delight. She pointed to a beautiful evergreen tree in front of the gypsy house. "Merry Christmas!" she cried.

The tree was an unusual gray-green with needles as soft as feathers. Fastened to its graceful branches were little packages tied in red, white and blue papers that looked as if they might have been picked up near the Halles. On top of the tree hung a copper star, like the patch the gypsies used for mending pots and pans.

"I bet that tree is the freshest, prettiest one in Paris," boasted Nikki. "I cut it down in the Jardin des Plantes only a few hours ago. And the sign near it said it is a very rare tree from India."

The gypsy children tore the little packages off the tree and gave them to the Calcets. They held nuts, candies and small celluloid toys.

"We like to give presents," said Tinka. "Perhaps that's because one of the Wise Men who brought gifts to the Christ Child was a gypsy."

"I never heard that before," said Suzy.

Tinka looked at her with chagrin. "What *did* you learn in your school besides those letters?" she asked.

But before Suzy could answer, Armand was presenting his carton of goodies to the gypsies. He generously added that it was from the Calcets too. But the biggest surprise was for him. Madame Calcet brought out a small package neatly wrapped in newspaper. A fragrant smell hovered around the gift. He opened it to find a glossy pink bar of soap. He looked at it for a long time. He sniffed it thoughtfully.

"Just what I need," he politely thanked her.

Chapter Eight

Old Armand found that he enjoyed the companionship of the gypsy camp. He liked to sit with his back against the fence watching Suzy teach the gypsy girls and Paul play games with the boys.

On the other hand, Suzy was not satisfied. She often frowned as she watched Paul and the boys. At last she brought her problem to the hobo.

"I'm worried about my brother," she confided in a grownup way. "He doesn't act like he belonged to our family any more. He's always playing with the gypsies, and he hardly ever comes near Evelyne and me. *We're* his family."

Armand had noticed this himself, but he tried to comfort Suzy. "Paul's a boy," he said, "so naturally he doesn't want to hang around girls all the time. You wouldn't want to put him in skirts, would you?"

But Suzy only pointed wrathfully across the courtyard. "Look!" she cried. "He even stands like a gypsy." Because Paul was idly standing on one leg with the other drawn up under him. He looked like a small stork.

"People have different ways of resting," Armand assured her. "Now, me, I lie down. That's the best way yet."

Paul himself didn't help matters. "I wish I were a gypsy," he told them one day. "I like the way they live. I wish I could go away with them in the spring."

Armand tried to reason with him. "If God wanted you to be a gypsy, He would have made you one," he said. "But He doesn't want everybody traipsing all over the country and living in tents. You don't want to spend your grownup life banging on tin pans, do you? Not when you have a smart sister like Suzy to teach you things."

Paul scowled and dug his toe into the sand. Armand smiled to see that his worn shoes were neatly capped with shining copper. Paul followed his look, then he smiled too. "The boys helped me mend my shoes," he explained. Then he ran away to join them.

"You see," said Suzy. "He's even learning how to work with copper."

Armand tried to think of something else to say to her, but his mouth only gaped open and his tongue stiffened.

A policeman was entering the yard. He was a stern-looking officer with a heavy coat and full-cut cape. His hat was pulled down over his thick eyebrows.

The gypsy boys, followed by Paul, disappeared into the tents. Most of the men were gone, but the few remaining ones vanished as quickly as the boys. Even the dogs, Jojo among them, tucked their tails between their legs and dived under the one automobile left in the yard.

Mireli rose from the steps of the van and went to meet the policeman. "Your fortune, monsieur?" she asked in her softest voice. "Let me tell your fortune. Perhaps there is a promotion waiting for you."

The policeman ignored her offer. "Is there a Nikki here?" he asked gruffly.

"No," said Mireli quickly. "He has gone."

"Where?" asked the policeman.

Mireli shrugged her shoulders. "He is out of town."

"When will he return?" persisted the man. "Tomorrow?"

"Who knows?" said Mireli vaguely. "Today is today and tomorrow may come late this year."

The policeman turned on his heel and stamped away.

Immediately the gypsy faces appeared in every tent opening. The dogs came slinking from under the car. The women gathered around Mireli. The men and children quickly joined them.

"They want to arrest Nikki," guessed one of the men.

"It must be because he cut down the Christmas tree," said Paul.

"They want to put him in the Army," wailed an old woman. "I know that is it. They put my Teodoro in the Army and he was never the same again. Gave up the wandering life and settled down in a house."

All the gypsies were upset. Without another word to each other, they began packing up their belongings and tearing down their tents. Petro grumbled when they started on his, but when he learned the reason, he awakened as if a pitcher of ice water had been thrown in his face.

"We can't leave until the rest of the men come home from the restaurants," said Mireli. She went to the opening and peered down the street.

The Calcet children watched the activity

with growing alarm. They had never seen the gypsies work so hard or so fast.

"You're going to leave!" cried Suzy.

"We always leave if the police visit us," said Tinka. "If we didn't, someone might be put in jail."

Mireli appealed to Armand. "Why don't you come with us?" she invited. "You and the Calcets? The skies are blue in Provence now and the flowers are blooming."

"I'll go with you," cried Paul with shining eyes. "I want to be a gypsy."

"No, no," cried Suzy, grabbing his arm. "We can't go off with the gypsies. We have to stay with mama. We're her children. "

Paul tore loose from her grasp. "I'm sick of being wet and cold," he said. "If I was a big man, I'd go to work and make enough money to buy us a house."

Suzy grabbed him again and angrily shook him. "You're always bragging about what you'd do if you were a big man," she retorted.

"You better begin thinking what you should do while you're a little boy."

"I'm going with the gypsies," repeated Paul, trying to pull away.

"Oh, Monsieur Armand," implored Suzy, "please don't let him go."

Armand gently put his hand on Paul's shoulder. "You can't go with them, boy," he said. "You've got to stay here with your family."

"Why can't I go?" asked Paul rebelliously. "Why do I have to stay here?"

Armand crossed his arms and stared down at the redheaded boy. "You can't go because—because—because you've got red hair," he said. "That's why."

"Why does that matter?" asked Paul.

"It matters plenty," answered Armand. "How far do you think the gypsies would get with a redheaded child? People would think they had kidnapped you. The police would put you in some strange home and the gypsies in jail."

A sudden thought darkened Suzy's blue

eyes. "We won't have any place to stay now," she said. "Do you think the new house will be ready for us in time, Monsieur Armand?"

Armand lowered his head in shame.

"If we could move there soon," said Paul, "I wouldn't want to go with the gypsies. I'd stay and help us move in."

"Will you take us to look at it?" Suzy begged the hobo. "Then we can see if it's almost finished."

Armand put his head between his hands. "There won't be any new house for you," he confessed. "It was all a mistake. It turned out the builders don't want children and dogs in it. You know how it is with a brand-new place? They want to keep it looking that way."

"No house for us?" cried Suzy with a catch in her voice. "Nothing?"

Armand couldn't look in her eyes. Paul darted away to the gypsies.

When the rest of the men returned, they were startled to hear about the policeman's unexpected visit. Nikki was upset by more than the call.

"And just at this unfortunate time when I've lost my wallet with all my week's earnings in it," he cried. "I know I lost it in the Café of the Laughing Frog. And the owner said he would have it returned to me if it were found."

"Humph!" grunted Armand. "Who would return a wallet full of money? Some people collect the stuff."

Petro tried to help. "We can use what I have in my pocket," he offered. "Then we will have to work along the way. I'm really wide awake now."

The little house on wheels was hooked to the back of one of the automobiles. The gypsies and their dogs piled over the seats. Jojo whined to go too because he had enjoyed his ride so much on Christmas Eve.

"We left one of the tents for you all," cried Nikki.

"There's almost another week due us on

the yard," Mireli added. "We've been paying rent to the wreckers."

The automobiles coughed and sputtered. Then they slowly ground through the sand toward the opening. The gypsies waved good-by. Tinka threw Suzy a kiss. Jojo tried to follow the cars, but Armand called him back. The little house on wheels which had been a home for Suzy and her mother and sister disappeared into the street.

There was nothing left to show that gypsies had ever lived in this yard. Nothing but a weather-beaten tent and the dead ashes of their fires.

Then those left behind noticed something else missing from the yard; There was no Paul. He was gone.

"He left with them," wailed Suzy. "Paul went off with the gypsies."

Evelyne began to howl. "I want Paul," she wept. "I want my brother."

"Oh, là, là," groaned Armand. "And there is still Madame to face."

He silently set to work getting a cold lunch for the children. The gypsies had left some cheese and bread in the tent. But nobody seemed hungry. Not even Jojo.

Armand felt that he was to blame for it all. He sat down with his back against the fence and thought and thought. Oh, oh, oh! It was all his fault. He had brought the children to the gypsies in the first place. But he had only tried to help them. That's what he got for ever having anything to do with starlings. Now he was caught in the same net with them. But was he? No. He could get up and go. He could push his buggy right through that opening in the fence and never come back.

At the thought, he rose to his feet and looked toward the opening. To his amazement, he saw a forlorn little figure come through it.

"Paul!" he shouted. "Is it really you, Paul?"

The boy nodded sadly, as if he wished it were somebody else.

"You left the gypsies and came back to us

because we're your family," cried Suzy joyously.

"I didn't go away with the gypsies," said the boy. "You're always saying I should stop bragging about what I'll do when I'm big and do something now. So I went down to the Halles and tried to get a job."

"Tried to get a job at the Halles?" asked Armand with fresh surprise.

"That funny tramp you knew said they needed pushers," Paul reminded him.

"You're too little to work," said Suzy. "You have to be big like Monsieur Armand."

The hobo uneasily tugged at his whiskers.

Paul looked at the copper toes on his shoes. "That's what all the men said," he continued. "They laughed at me. They showed me a big cart full of boxes and told me that if I could push it, I could have a job." Paul wiped his eyes with his knuckles. "I pushed and pushed, but I couldn't even budge it. Then they all laughed at me again."

Armand was indignant. "The nerve of them!" he exclaimed. "I'll go down there tomorrow morning and hang them all up on those hooks. I'll—"

But he didn't finish his threats. He was frightened to see the policeman coming in again. Oh, oh, this must have something to do with Paul's visit to the Halles. Perhaps they had got wind of these vagabond children and the policeman was coming to take them away. Oh, oh, oh, they should have gone with the gypsies.

But the policeman looked bewildered. "Weren't there gypsies in this yard?" he asked.

"They had to leave suddenly," said Armand. "Received word of a sick relative in Normandy."

"And I suppose the one named Nikki left with them," added the policeman.

"Of course," said Armand. "It was his relative who was sick."

The policeman pursed his lips and shook his head. "Too bad!" he said. "A wallet lost by him was found under a table at the Café of the Laughing Frog. Too bad!" He pulled a new leather wallet from a pocket under his cape. "And in it is the lucky ticket that won yesterday's lottery. Too bad! It is a shame!"

Armand's eyes brightened. "I'll keep the wallet for him," he offered.

The policeman eyed him suspiciously. His sharp eyes saw Armand's unkempt whiskers and ragged tramp clothes. He tucked the wallet under his cape again.

"1 can't deliver it to anyone but the rightful owner," he said.

Then he turned and walked away, shaking his head and muttering, "Too bad! Too bad!"

Armand exploded with a roar. "Too bad indeed!" he roared. "I call it a tragedy to lose that nice new wallet."

"And all the money," said Suzy.

"And the lucky ticket," added Paul.

"Pouh!" said Armand. "What would Nikki do with so much money? It might ruin his character. But anybody would hate to lose that wallet. It's just the right size for carrying around the coins a man needs."

"What will we do now?" worried Suzy.

"We won't have any place to live after this week."

"Mama will cry," said Evelyne solemnly.

"I wish I could have moved that cart," said Paul. "I tried so hard."

A great feeling of shame came over Armand at the boy's words. The children's eyes were turned to him with that needful look.

He cleared his throat. "Everything is going to turn out all right," he assured them. "I'm going to get a steady job. Your mama and I ought to make enough between us to rent that room in Clichy for you nestlings."

Then, frightened by his own brave words, he slumped to the ground and leaned back weakly against the wall.

Chapter Nine

Madame Calcet was the most surprised of all when she heard that
Armand planned to take a regular
job.

"I can't let you do that," she said. "It
would not be fair."

For a few seconds Armand was ready to
agree with her. Oh, là, là! To settle down to
work after all these lazy years! But, there were
the children with their pleading eyes.

"It would be the fairest thing in Paris,"
persisted Armand, half-arguing with himself.
"We put our money together to pay rent, and
with what is left over we eat. You cook my

107

meals and give me a corner to live in. Suzy can draw a square on the floor."

"But you shouldn't have to help us," said Madame Calcet. "We aren't even related to you."

The children disagreed.

"He's our grandpa," cried Suzy.

"He's the only grandpa we have," said Paul.

"Grandpapa, grandpapa," sang Evelyne.

"Do I have to beg for grandchildren?" Armand asked Madame Calcet. "To tell you the truth, I'm beginning to be ashamed of begging. It takes away a man's self-respect."

Madame Calcet had to give in. There were too many against her.

Once she had agreed, she became very practical.

"If you are going to look for work," she said, "you must look respectable. One who seeks a job tries to look his best."

"How do I do that?" asked Armand.

"First you take a bath," she told him.

"A bath!" exclaimed Armand in alarm. "At this time of the year?"

"It will be warm enough in the tent because it is near the bakery wall," she said. "I will heat water in a pot over the fire. Then you can take a bird bath in there."

"I'll die of pneumonia," he declared.

"You will be a new man," she promised. Even while he made excuse after excuse, she built up the fire and brought water from the street hydrant. "There, now," she said when the water was boiling. "It is time for you to use that pink soap. I did not give it to you to eat."

So Armand carried the water into the tent, fussing and fuming all the while. "Come, Jojo," he called the dog. "You can chase the soap when it slips out of my hands."

"And throw your clothes out," called Madame Calcet after him. "Suzy and I will sponge the spots and I will mend the holes and tears."

She went to work on Armand's old clothes.

She hung them on the fence and beat them. She and Suzy sponged the stains and spots as best they could. Evelyne made herself busy brushing his worn beret.

"And he can wear that other pair of shoes in his buggy," said Paul. "The gypsies and I mended the soles with copper to surprise him."

They could hear moans and groans coming from the tent. Then they heard Jojo howling.

"Oh, I hope they didn't spill hot water over themselves," said Suzy.

"Perhaps Jojo ate the pretty soap," said Evelyne.

To their astonishment, a strange beast came bounding from the tent to them. It was a dripping-wet beast but a very white one. It was Jojo looking as if he had fallen into a bucket of whitewash.

Suzy grabbed him before he could roll in the sand. "He's white, mama!" she cried in amazement. "He's really a white dog."

She took a clean rag and pulled him over

to the fire. She rubbed and rubbed him dry. His long fur fluffed out like duckling fuzz.

Evelyne kept asking, "Where is Jojo? Where is our Jojo?"

Paul brought Armand's clothes and shoes to him. When the man came out of the tent, he looked as changed as Jojo. Like the dog's fur, his whiskers were soft and fluffy. And he had a damp look.

Suzy was enchanted with his bearded chin. "I'll trim it for you," she offered.

Obediently Armand sat on a slab of concrete and Suzy went to work with her mother's scissors. She snipped and snipped.

"I made a mistake in the middle," she said, "so I'll have to make two points." She frowned and snipped some more. From one side to the other she moved, snipping with the scissors. At last she was satisfied.

"You look so distinguished," said Madame Calcet in admiration.

"Just like an artist," added Suzy admiringly.

"Why do you have to dress up to get a job as a pusher at the Halles?" asked Paul. "They didn't look like that."

"Tatata!" exclaimed Armand. "You don't think I'm going to apply for a low job like that, do you?"

"Are you going to be a policeman?" asked Evelyne.

"No, indeed," replied Armand. "Don't you remember my friend Father Christmas said somebody was looking for a night watchman? That's the job for me. Rest all day and take a couple walks around some building during the night. And once I get Jojo trained, I won't even have to do that."

"But no one will be able to see you at night," said Suzy in disappointment. "They won't be able to see your stylish whiskers."

Armand laughed at this as he walked toward the opening. Then he called to Jojo. "Come, boy," he called. "Part of this job will belong to you too."

He walked slowly in the direction of the

Louvre store. His copper soles clinked against cobbles and asphalt. He didn't want to hurry to a job. Goodness, no! He might change his mind at the last minute.

"Now, what was the name of the man who was looking for the watchman?" he asked Jojo. "Hum! Hum! Camille won't be there any more. Monsieur—Monsieur—? I have caught it. Latour! Monsieur Latour!"

His steps clinked faster, and the fluffy white dog pranced at his heels.

The Rue de Rivoli was busy as a beehive again. Hadn't those people bought all they needed? But the Christmas decorations were gone. Now the vendors were screaming about the New Year.

Armand helped Jojo through the glass doors of which the store was so proud. He walked to a saleslady.

"Is there a Monsieur Latour here?" he asked.

"He's on the mezzanine now," she answered. "Oh, no. Here he comes. Monsieur Latour! Monsieur Latour!"

Armand turned to face the haughty floor-walker. His first idea was to grab Jojo in his arms and run through the glass doors again. But the haughty monsieur did not recognize them.

Somehow the new Armand found his voice. "Camille who worked here Christmas told me that you were looking for a night watchman, monsieur," he said.

Monsieur Latour tapped his forehead, trying to remember something. He kept looking at Armand in a puzzled way.

"Oh, yes, a friend wants someone dependable to look after his building," he answered. "But haven't I met you somewhere before? Your face looks familiar."

"Perhaps we were at the same concert," said Armand. "Has your friend found a man yet?"

Monsieur Latour kept staring at him. Then he noticed Jojo. His face cleared. "I think I remember now," he said. "It was at a dog show somewhere."

"Probably," answered Armand. "Jojo has won lots of blue ribbons at them. But the job—"

"Ah, yes," said the floorwalker. "I'll write down the address for you. It isn't far from here. And ask for Monsieur Brunot!"

He took a small folded bag from the counter and wrote the address with a flourish. He handed it to Armand. "Just off the Rue de l'Opéra," he said.

Armand pocketed the bag and hurried out of the store before the floorwalker's memory could improve. He crossed the street and went through the arcades of the Théâtre-Français with its grimy walls and pillars. He looked at the square, where sycamore trees were bare and the two fountains dry.

"It will be a nice place for me to loaf on spring days," he said to Jojo. Already he could see green trees and hear the splashing of the fountains.

A woman wearing a fur coat and a feather hat came parading down the Rue de l'Opéra with a black poodle. The poodle wore a green plaid coat and fur-topped bootees. It stopped to sniff at Jojo as if to say, "Haven't we met at some dog show?" But the woman jerked at its leash.

Armand strolled down the Rue de l'Opéra with such dignity that his shoes scarcely made a sound. On both sides were fashionable shops with windows made up to attract wealthy shoppers. At the very end stood the magnificent opera house with its green dome and the graceful statues on its roof.

Armand pulled out the bag and looked at it. Then he turned down the next side street. It was a narrow, hidden street and the stores on each side were much humbler than those on the Rue de l'Opéra.

Armand studied the number on the bag. He matched it with the one on a wooden arch over a broken gate.

He turned into a shabby brick-paved courtyard. It was closed in by the blank walls of three tall buildings. Through the years they had been patched with bricks of different colors. One wall was so old and crooked that it was held up by great wooden props. Directly across from the gate, the lower wall was divided into stores even dingier than those in the narrow street.

And not far from the entrance, a glassed-in cubbyhole was built into the wall. Two men came out of it now. One went into the store advertising secondhand radio parts. The other, a lean man wearing spectacles, approached Armand.

"Can you tell me where I can find Monsieur Brunot?" asked Armand, sweeping his beret from his head.

"You are looking at him," answered the man with good humor.

Then Armand showed him the writing on the bag and explained his mission. "I should like the job of night watchman, monsieur," he said, "if it isn't filled yet. I have eyes like a cat in the dark."

The man corrected him. "It is not a night

watchman we want," he said, "but a care-
taker. You know, someone dependable to give
the tenants their keys, distribute the mail and
put out the trash cans early each morning."

Armand blinked. This was a different kettle
from the one he had been sold. The job sounded
as if there was some work attached to it.

Monsieur Brunot noticed his hesitation.
"We really want a family man," he said.

That brought Armand's mind back to the
needy Calcets. "Oh, I've got a family all right,
monsieur," he said. "Three children and their
mother. You should see my grandchildren.
They would steal your heart away."

The man looked pleased. He even scratched
Jojo's ears. "And a dog," he added to Armand's
family. "What's your name?"

"Armand Pouly," said the other without
any hesitation. "And I've never been one to
fear work."

"The work isn't so hard," said Monsieur
Brunot, "but it ties one down. That's why the
last man left."

"Oh, I'm already right well tied down by my family," Armand assured him.

"And the pay is low," added Monsieur Brunot, "but that's because of the living quarters that go with the job."

"Living quarters?" asked Armand, perking up.

"Right through the door here," said the man. He led Armand into the cubbyhole and down some steps. He opened another door. "Three rooms," he went on. "Small, of course, and the light is poor, but they're dry and there's running water in the kitchen."

He snapped on a dim light and Armand looked at each room in turn, as if he were very particular about where his family lived.

The paint was peeling off the walls and the few pieces of furniture were worn down to the bone. The kitchen stove was rusted and the linoleum on the floors cracked and faded. But even as he looked, Armand saw the rooms change in front of his eyes.

As if by magic, the walls brightened with a

new coat of paint. Lace curtains appeared at the small, high windows. He walked over the floors carefully, as if not to disturb the woven rugs which would replace the linoleum.

The splintered table-top disappeared under a checked cloth. Suzy was sitting by it, studying her books. The stove began to crackle as Madame Calcet stood over it stirring the soup. And there was Evelyne climbing the high stool to look out of the window. Paul was playing with Jojo in the courtyard.

"It isn't walls and furniture that make a home," Armand told Monsieur Brunot. "It's the family." Then he added, "Monsieur Latour said to tell you that he recommended me highly."

"I can see by your appearance that you are sober and industrious, Pouly," said Monsieur Brunot, "and that is enough for me. Do you think you could get moved in by tomorrow? That doesn't give you much time, but I'd like to be free for New Year's Day."

New Year's Day! Tomorrow night would

be New Year's Eve. It would find the Calcets and himself beginning a new life as well.

"We can move in this afternoon, monsieur," said Armand. "The children's mother has the day off today. And we don't have much fancy bric-a-brac to move."

Monsieur Brunot explained some of his duties. There were the keys hanging in the cubbyhole. They belonged to the rooms over the stores. Be sure the tenants didn't walk off with them. He must close and lock the gate at night and open it early in the morning. Perhaps Madame would help him with the keys and roomers. A woman was so necessary in a job like this. That is why he hadn't taken the last two men who applied.

Oh, that would suit Madame Calcet to a hair. Now she could give up her job in the laundry and stay home to look after her children and the roomers. She would be earning her own way. That would make her happy.

The two men shook hands. As he turned to go, Armand noticed the twisted trunk of an old wisteria vine in the corner. Come spring, a vine that big would be covering the ugly blind walls with blossoms. The courtyard would be a garden.

At last he was on his long way to where the Calcets were waiting. Jojo barked happily at his heels as if his eyes, too, had seen the way the rooms and the courtyard would look in the future.

Armand walked briskly. He raised his head so that the points of his beard were thrust forward. He straightened his shoulders in the mended coat. He wasn't a hobo any more. He was a workingman of Paris.

The End